Juv
623.74
B413
2015

READY FOR MILITARY ACTION

POWERFUL MILITARY VEHICLES

by Samantha S. Bell

Content Consultant
Mitchell A. Yockelson
Adjunct Faculty
US Naval Academy

Core Library
An Imprint of Abdo Publishing
www.abdopublishing.com

www.abdopublishing.com

Published by Abdo Publishing, a division of ABDO, PO Box 398166, Minneapolis, Minnesota 55439. Copyright © 2015 by Abdo Consulting Group, Inc. International copyrights reserved in all countries. No part of this book may be reproduced in any form without written permission from the publisher. Core Library™ is a trademark and logo of Abdo Publishing.

Printed in the United States of America, North Mankato, Minnesota
092014
012015

Cover Photo: Haraz N. Ghanbari/AP Images
Interior Photos: Haraz N. Ghanbari/AP Images, 1; Cpl. Tyler Hill/US Department of Defense, 4; Cpl. Jeremy Vought/AP Images, 7; Mass Communication Specialist 3rd Class James Turner/Official U.S. Navy, 9, 45; Library of Congress, 12, 15; Joint Service Audiovisual Team/Defense Imagery, 17; Peter Dejong/AP Images, 20; The U.S. Army, 24; Sgt Randall M. Yackiel/Wikimedia, 26; Staff Sgt. Alfred Johnson/US Department of Defense, 29; Cpl. Artur Shvartsberg/US Department of Defense, 32; Tech. Sgt. Michael R. Holzworth/US Department of Defense, 35; William D. Moss/US Department of Defense, 37; Wikimedia, 39; Shutterstock Images, 40; Staff Sgt. Aaron Allmon/US Department of Defense, 42; Mohammed Jalil/AP Images, 43

Editor: Patrick Donnelly
Series Designer: Becky Daum

Library of Congress Control Number: 2014944244

Cataloging-in-Publication Data
Bell, Samantha S.
 Powerful military vehicles / Samantha S. Bell.
   p. cm. -- (Ready for military action)
ISBN 978-1-62403-654-5 (lib. bdg.)
Includes bibliographical references and index.
1. Armored vehicles, Military--Juvenile literature. 2. Transportation, Military--Juvenile literature. 3. Vehicles, Military--Juvenile literature.   I. Title.
623.74--dc23

2014944244

CONTENTS

CHAPTER ONE
Into Enemy Fire **4**

CHAPTER TWO
Early Military Vehicles **12**

CHAPTER THREE
Vehicles with Tracks **20**

CHAPTER FOUR
Wheeled Vehicles **32**

Top Missions. 42

Stop and Think 44

Glossary 46

Learn More. 47

Index 48

About the Author 48

CHAPTER ONE

INTO ENEMY FIRE

On March 25, 2003, a convoy of US military vehicles made its way toward Baghdad, Iraq. Marines in tanks, Humvees, Amphibious Assault Vehicles, trucks, and other vehicles moved through the flat desert. But then the landscape began to change. The marines noticed a large embankment along the road to the right. The enemy sometimes created these embankments as a defense. This time,

The Humvee has been a versatile and useful vehicle for the US military in Iraq and Afghanistan.

that was the case. The enemy was hiding behind the embankment, waiting to attack the marines.

First Lieutenant Brian Chontosh was riding in a Humvee with four other marines. Lance Corporal Robert Kerman was also riding, Corporal Armand McCormick was driving, Corporal Thomas Franklin manned the gun, and Lance Corporal Ken Korte operated the radio. Chontosh suspected trouble. He told Franklin to keep the gun pointed at the embankment. The lieutenant was right. Within moments, the convoy was ambushed. Enemy bombs, grenades, and automatic weapons fire rained down on them. Four tanks were in front of

A Military Favorite

The Humvee was designed to carry personnel and light cargo. It has a crew of two to four soldiers, and it can carry up to eight more troops. Even with a full human load, there's still room for a machine gun. Manufactured in the United States by AM General, Humvees are used throughout the US military. More than 60 other allied countries also have purchased Humvees from AM General.

Marine Captain Brian Chontosh, right, stands with General Michael Hagee after Chontosh received the Navy Cross.

Honoring Our Heroes

For his incredible bravery in the face of overwhelming odds, Brian Chontosh was awarded the Navy Cross, one of the highest honors a serviceman can receive. Armand McCormick and Robert Kerman both received the Silver Star. Thomas Franklin and Ken Korte were later awarded Navy and Marine Corps Commendation Medals.

Chontosh's Humvee. They were blocking the road ahead. His platoon was trapped in a kill zone, an area where many soldiers lose their lives.

A Bold Move

Then Chontosh saw an opening in the embankment. He told McCormick to steer the Humvee into the trench, right into enemy fire. Franklin was still at the gun. He started shooting, destroying an enemy machine gun bunker. As he continued to fire, Chontosh, McCormick, and Kerman jumped out of the Humvee. Franklin kept shooting from the vehicle while Korte used the radio to warn the rest of the troops.

A Humvee drives to shore after launching from a landing craft utility vehicle.

Chontosh led the others down the trench, firing as they went. When he ran out of ammunition, he used his pistol. Out of bullets again, Chontosh picked up an enemy weapon and continued to shoot. When that one was empty, he picked up another one. Finally, McCormick handed Chontosh an enemy grenade launcher. He fired, sending a fireball through the trench. The enemy was forced to clear out. In 15 minutes, the attack was over. The marine convoy continued on to Baghdad. Without the sturdy and reliable Humvee, they likely would not have made it out of the kill zone alive.

Even though the convoy was ambushed, the troops survived because their vehicles were equipped for battle. With just a Humvee and some weapons, the four marines were able to repel the enemy. With many other powerful vehicles in the US military, today's soldiers are well prepared to do even more.

STRAIGHT TO THE SOURCE

In 2010 Brian Chontosh described some of the events that occurred the day his convoy was ambushed:

> "We're caught in the contact zone, the kill zone," Chontosh said. "Tanks started moving forward to try to get out of the kill zone. I'd like to sit here today, nine years later, and connect all the dots . . . but more or less things just started happening."
>
> McCormick put his foot on the gas.
>
> "I was going as fast as I could go," McCormick said. "Finally, we found an opening in the berm."
>
> He steered the vehicle almost directly into the center of a defended enemy trench. Franklin immediately destroyed the enemy machine gun bunkers there with the .50-caliber machine gun.

Source: Jennifer Hlad. "They Were Probably the Most Horrific Days of My Life." Stars and Stripes. www.stripes.com, May 31, 2012. Web. Accessed August 14, 2014.

Consider Your Audience

Read this passage carefully. The audience for this newspaper is military personnel and their families. How would you adapt the story for a different audience, such as your teacher, your friends, or a younger sibling? Rewrite the story conveying the same information for the new audience. How does your new approach differ from the original story? Why?

CHAPTER TWO

EARLY MILITARY VEHICLES

The US military uses vehicles of all shapes and sizes to move people, transport equipment, and locate and fight enemy forces. From mountain to desert to jungle, these jeeps, tanks, and trucks are built to travel over all kinds of landscapes. But the military did not always rely on vehicles. For centuries, armies used horses, mules, oxen, and wagons to transport troops and equipment. That began to

The US military purchased thousands of Model T Fords to use during World War I.

change in the mid-1800s, however, as steam engines came into use. Steam tractors hauled heavy guns and supplies, though they moved very slowly. In 1885 Karl Benz of Germany developed the first automobile powered by gasoline. Within 30 years, motor vehicles would be used in a war.

World War I Vehicles

In the late 1800s Americans began designing and manufacturing automobiles. One of the most popular cars was Henry Ford's Model T. When the United States entered World War I (1914–1918) in 1917, Ford agreed to sell the cars to the US military and its allies. Thousands of Model Ts were used as staff cars, ambulances, vans, and cargo trucks. The top speed for the Model T was 45 miles per hour (72 km/h). That was much faster than the troops could have traveled by foot or on horseback.

Another popular vehicle of World War I was the Nash Quad. As indicated by its name, the Nash Quad was one of the first four-wheel-drive vehicles. That

President Franklin D. Roosevelt reviews US troops from an army jeep during World War II.

means all four of its wheels were connected to the engine. It handled well on the rough roads, traveling at 15 miles per hour (24 km/h). A bench seat provided enough room for the driver and one passenger. Behind them was a truck bed for carrying supplies.

Versatile and Valuable

During World War II (1939–1945) the US Army needed a small, four-wheel-drive transport vehicle for reconnaissance. Soon the jeep was used by all branches of the military. It had no doors, and many of them had removable canvas roofs. Its simple engine generated enough power for the jeep to go 65 miles per hour (105 km/h). Some jeeps carried officers. Others carried supplies such as ammunition, food, and water. Some carried wounded soldiers to first-aid stations. Others were mounted with machine guns or covered with armor. In just four years more than 640,000 jeeps were produced by Willys-Overland Motors and Ford Motor Company.

What's in a Name?

No one really knows how the jeep got its name. Some think it was named after a cartoon character called Eugene the Jeep. Others believe it came from the initials "GP," which may have stood for "general purpose." Another guess is that it came from a World War I slang term for untested equipment. Because it was quiet enough to use as a reconnaissance vehicle, the army actually preferred the name "peep." Then, in 1941, a reporter asked a test driver what it was called. He said it was a "jeep." The name was used in advertisements, and it finally stuck.

Soldiers on patrol with a Mechanical Mule

Half-track vehicles were also introduced during World War II. The name describes these vehicles perfectly. The front half of the vehicle had wheels, while the back wheels rolled on tracks like a tank. All of the half-track vehicles had some type of armor depending on how they were used. Some were used for transporting soldiers. Others were equipped with machine guns and other weapons.

With the 1950s came the Mechanical Mule, a popular vehicle with soldiers and marines throughout the Vietnam War (1954–1975). It had one seat for

17

The Mighty Mite

In the 1950s the marines needed a new kind of jeep. It had to be light enough to be carried by helicopter along with supplies and personnel. It also had to be easy to maneuver and maintain. The result was the Mighty Mite. It had a self-cooling engine, and its aluminum body kept it light. Because it was small, it could go deep into the jungle. The Mighty Mite was so well balanced it could drive on a flat road on just three wheels. It was used in Vietnam until a new type of helicopter was produced that could carry a full-sized jeep.

the driver and a platform for transporting troops and equipment. Like a mule, it was sturdy and dependable. This four-wheel-drive vehicle was strong enough to carry up to 1,000 pounds (454 kg). But it was light enough to be lifted by helicopters and dropped by parachute. When wrapped in a canvas, it could be used as a boat to cross a river.

Around the same time, the army started using the M35 cargo truck. It was produced from 1950 until 1988. The M35 was built to carry 5,000 pounds (2,300 kg) of cargo off road and 10,000 pounds (4,500 kg) on road. Other versions of this versatile vehicle were used as tow trucks, medical vans, dump trucks, and guided-missile launchers.

New military vehicles continue to be developed. Current vehicles continue to be improved. Manufacturers are constantly trying to find ways to make them better. Military vehicles must transport soldiers, carry equipment and supplies, and serve as weapons. And they must do those jobs while keeping the troops as safe as possible.

EXPLORE ONLINE

The focus of Chapter Two is the history and development of military vehicles. The jeep was introduced during World War II. The website below also focuses on jeeps used during that war. As you know, every source is different. How is the information in the website different from the information in this chapter? How is it the same? What can you learn from this website?

World War II Jeeps Today
www.mycorelibrary.com/vehicles

CHAPTER THREE

VEHICLES WITH TRACKS

While many early military vehicles moved on wheels, others were later developed that also ran on tracks. These "caterpillar tracks" are made up of metal plates that are linked together. Because they are larger than wheels, the tracks can carry more weight and provide better traction. They also help the vehicles move on soft ground without getting stuck or sinking.

The Abrams has been the US Army's main combat tank since 1980.

Superior Fighting Vehicles

The Abrams tanks were some of the strongest vehicles during the Gulf War (1990–1991). Out of the 1,848 tanks in service, only 18 were taken out because of damage. Mechanics were able to repair nine of those. The tanks kept the soldiers safe as well. Throughout all the battles, not a single Abrams crewman was killed.

Abrams Main Battle Tank

One powerful vehicle with tracks is the Abrams main battle tank. One of the most advanced tanks in the world, it has been the US Army's main combat tank since 1980. The Abrams tank is more than 32 feet (10 m) long and 16 feet (5 m) wide. It weighs approximately 63 short tons (57 metric tons). That is more than nine elephants. Yet it is still easy to maneuver. It uses the same kind of engine found in helicopters and airplanes. The tank can move along at 42 miles per hour (68 km/h). The engine is reliable, easy to maintain, and very quiet. It fires up with just the push of a button.

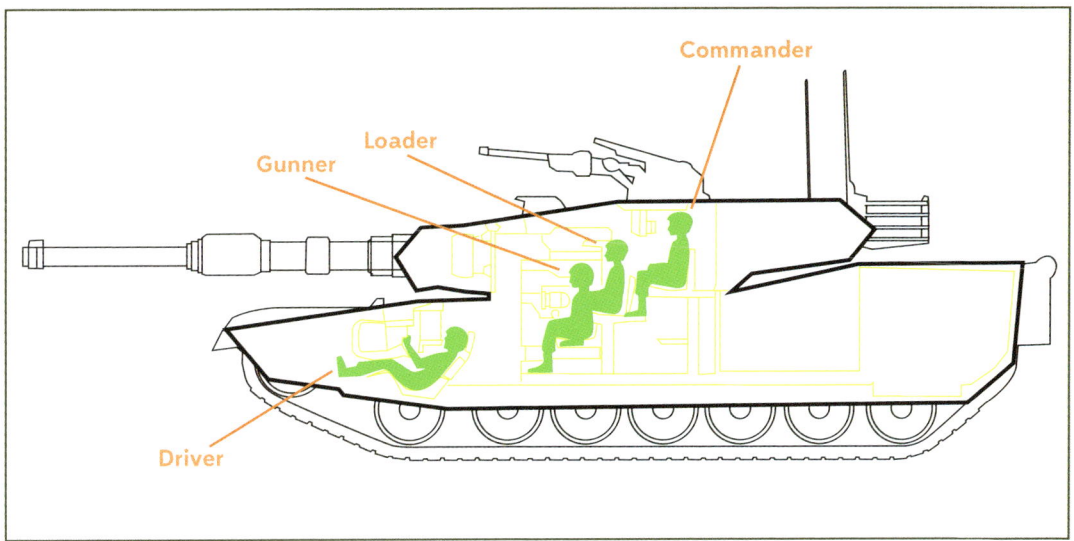

The Abrams M1 Battle Tank
The diagram shows the inside of an Abrams battle tank. Notice where the crew is stationed. After reading about the tank, what did you think it looked like? How has that idea changed? How does seeing the inside of the tank help you better understand how it works?

The Abrams is operated by four soldiers. The commander directs the movements of the tank, including where to go, what ammunition to use, and when to fire. The driver steers the tank. The loader finds and loads the correct ammunition, and the gunner fires it. The soldiers are protected by layers of armor on the outside of the tank. The armor contains depleted uranium, a substance that is more than twice

The Abrams tank has been useful in all types of terrain. Here, a group of Abrams tanks heads into battle in Kuwait.

as dense as steel. That provides an extra layer of protection in combat.

Many improvements have been made to the Abrams tank over the years. In the late 1980s the army introduced the M1A2 model. It featured improved armor, a larger gun, satellite navigation, and communication equipment to send information to aircraft. It also featured the new NBC system, which protects soldiers from nuclear, biological, and chemical warfare. It has an air cleaning system, a radiation warning device, and a chemical agent detector. The crew also has protective suits and face masks.

The Abrams tanks were very effective in desert conditions found in Iraq and Afghanistan during the last two decades. Their advanced imaging system helped crews find their targets in the dark. It also cut through smoke clouds and dust storms. Most other tanks have to stop to shoot at a target. But the Abrams can fire while on the move. The tank's rounds race toward a target at approximately 1 mile (1.6 km) per second. The tanks are so accurate they can destroy a building 2.5 miles (4 km) away.

Bradley Infantry Fighting Vehicles

In addition to needing vehicles that carry powerful weapons, the military must have a way to transport soldiers safely. During the 1980s a new type of personnel carrier was introduced. Not only did it protect the soldiers, but it also was fast and loaded with firepower. This new infantry fighting vehicle,

Two M3 Bradley vehicles await their orders.

the M2 Bradley, proved to be so effective that it is still being used today.

The Bradley vehicles have a three-person crew, including the commander, the driver, and the gunner. The M2 can also carry six to seven troops. The M3 Bradley cavalry fighting vehicle is designed for reconnaissance. It carries the crew and two scouts. The scouts observe enemy troops and report what they see.

The Bradleys are fully armored. They shield the troops from artillery and small arms fire, or shots from handheld weapons, on all sides. With their powerful engines, the Bradleys move fast enough to keep up with the Abrams battle tanks. But they do much more than carry troops from place to place.

The Bradleys are designed to fight the enemy. They have enough firepower to destroy enemy tanks and other vehicles that threaten the troops. The main weapon on the Bradley is the chain gun. It can fire 200 rounds per minute and has a range of approximately 2,200 yards (2,000 m). A machine gun is mounted beside the chain gun. Bradleys are also supplied with two antitank missile

General Bradley

The Bradley Fighting Vehicles were named to honor General Omar Nelson Bradley, one of the great leaders of World War II. He commanded US troops in North Africa, Sicily, Normandy, and Germany. His last command, the 12th US Army Group, was the largest group ever to serve under a single commander. Bradley's concern for his men earned him the nickname "the soldier's general." Even after he retired, military and political leaders continued to ask him for advice.

launchers. The missiles can hit and disable a tank from more than two miles (3.2 km) away. The M2 carries seven missiles, and the M3 can carry up to 12.

M88A2 HERCULES

Even though they have armor and weapons, large fighting vehicles are sometimes damaged during combat. That's when a recovery vehicle joins in the mission. One such vehicle is the M88A2 Heavy Equipment Recovery Combat Utility Lift and Evacuation System, or HERCULES. Its job is to recover disabled vehicles, even while under fire. It also helps vehicles that are stuck or overturned to get back on the battlefield. Sometimes the crew fixes a disabled vehicle in the field. Other times they tow the vehicle to a maintenance unit.

The first M88 HERCULES was built in 1961. More improvements led to the M88A1 in 1973. These were equipped with diesel engines, as well as the NBC protection system. They were built especially to support the Abrams battle tanks. However, it took

The M88 HERCULES is the army's top large vehicle for support and recovery missions.

two M88A1 vehicles to tow just one tank. In 1997, the stronger M88A2 HERCULES was introduced.

The M88A2 has more power than earlier models. It can recover vehicles that weigh up to 70 short tons (63.5 metric tons), including the Abrams battle tanks. It has a 35-foot (11-m) boom, a metal arm that is used to lift parts of the tank's engine out for repair. It also has a winch with 280 feet (85 m) of cable. The winch can pull 140,000 pounds (63,500 kg). It is strong enough to pull a tank from the mud or drag a disabled tank to a safe area for repair.

The recovery vehicle carries a three-person crew that includes the commander, the operator, and the mechanic. The armor on the M88A2 shields the crew from artillery fragments, small arms fire, and antipersonnel mines. The NBC system protects them from nuclear, biological, and chemical weapons. The M88A2 also has smoke screen generators. These produce large smoke clouds to give the troops extra cover when needed. A machine gun with 1,300 rounds provides further protection.

STRAIGHT TO THE SOURCE

One of the goals of the US military in Iraq was to train the Iraqi Army to protect its own country. The following excerpt is from an article that describes some of this training involving the M88A2 HERCULES:

> The M88A2 OPNET course gives the students in-depth classroom training on the recovery vehicle, along with hands-on opportunities to grasp the concepts taught during the 55-day course.
>
> "We are given step-by-step directions on the M88A2," said Iraqi Army Major Kasam with the Iraqi Armor Engineering School in Taji, Iraq.
>
> "When the course is over, those assets (M88A2s) will be turned over to the Iraqi Army for their use," said Lieutenant Colonel David C. Beachman.
>
> "It was a very proud moment when we received this equipment," Kasam said.
>
> Source: US Army Specialist Breeanna J. DuBuke. "BCTC Course Plays Key Role in Iraqi Army's Future." Official Homepage of the United States Army. www.army.mil, April 2, 2011. Web. Accessed August 13, 2014.

What's the Big Idea?

What is the main point of the article? Pick out two details that make this point. What can you tell about the Iraqi Army based on this article? What can you tell about the US military?

CHAPTER FOUR

WHEELED VEHICLES

Tracks help heavy vehicles move along, but wheels help lighter vehicles go even faster. These vehicles vary in size, firepower, and levels of protection, and they all fill important roles in the US military.

The Humvee

The High Mobility Multipurpose Wheeled Vehicle, or Humvee, was introduced into service in 1983. Fast

A soldier in a Humvee crosses a stream in Afghanistan.

and reliable, Humvees have taken over many of the roles of smaller vehicles such as the jeep. They can serve as transport vehicles, missile platforms, special operations vehicles, and ambulances.

Humvees travel up to 65 miles per hour (105 km/h), and they can handle all types of terrain. They ride just 16 inches (41 cm) off the ground, giving them good balance. But they weren't designed to provide much protection. Earlier models didn't have armor. Those vehicles had no defense against enemy attacks.

But sometimes the Humvees have to be used in combat. Variations have been developed to add protection for the troops. One model includes a fully armored passenger area with bullet-resistant glass windows. Other changes include more powerful engines, better brakes, and improved cooling systems.

Soldiers dismount from an M1126 Stryker.

Stryker Infantry Carrier Vehicle

In the late 1990s the military wanted to send out troops that would be ready for several different types of missions. This required a vehicle with protective armor that could be deployed quickly. The result was the M1126 Stryker Infantry Carrier Vehicle.

Introduced in 2002, the Stryker was the US Army's first new armored vehicle in more than 20 years. It has enough armor to protect the troops it carries, but it is still light enough to be transported in an aircraft. The Stryker has eight wheels, though it usually runs

The FANG Challenge

In 2013 the Defense Advanced Research Projects Agency (DARPA) held a new kind of contest. They called it the Fast Adaptable Next-Generation Ground Vehicle (FANG) Challenge. Americans were invited to create a design for a new combat vehicle that could travel on land and in water. Any American could enter, either as an individual or as part of a team. The purpose of the contest was to see how well DARPA's new online design tools worked. The winning team shared a prize of $1 million.

in four-wheel drive. It can travel up to 62 miles per hour (100 km/h).

The Stryker Infantry Carrier holds nine troops along with the two-person crew. It is armed with a machine gun and a grenade launcher. The weapons protect the troops during transport. They also allow the crew to fire on the enemy as the troops dismount.

Variations of the Stryker Infantry Carrier have been created to fill other roles. Some of these roles include reconnaissance and medical evacuation.

The MRAP is designed to help protect troops from mines and IEDs.

Mine Resistant Ambush Protected Vehicle

Many military vehicles protect soldiers from small arms fire. But most are still at risk against improvised explosive devices (IEDs). These homemade bombs can blast through the bottom of the vehicles, causing many casualties. The military needed a vehicle that would provide better protection. The solution came in 2006 with the Mine Resistant Ambush Protected (MRAP) vehicle. Its unique design shields the soldiers from blasts directly below the vehicle.

Desert Patrol Vehicles

US Navy SEALs have an off-road vehicle known for its speed and agility. This Desert Patrol Vehicle is a military dune buggy that can go twice as fast as a Humvee over open terrain. It has room for up to three crewmembers and a variety of weapons. With the Desert Patrol Vehicle, SEALs can perform rescue operations, light-strike missions, and deep reconnaissance.

Like other armored vehicles, the MRAP safeguards troops from small arms fire. But unlike other vehicles, it has a V-shaped hull. The shape helps deflect the force of an IED blast. The MRAP also has layers of thick armored glass. It has a blast-resistant underbody for even more protection.

The MRAP can travel over all types of terrain. It rides high off the ground for better mobility. These vehicles are used in a variety of roles, including convoy escort, troop transport, tow truck, and ambulance. They are also used to dispose of explosives and clear mines. Of all the wheeled vehicles, the MRAP is the one chosen for

The Desert Patrol Vehicle is a speedy military dune buggy used by Navy SEALs.

the most dangerous combat operations. The military's original plan was to build only a few thousand MRAPs. But because they have worked so well, more than 27,000 have been put to use. They are employed by all the branches of the military, as well as the Special Operations Command.

39

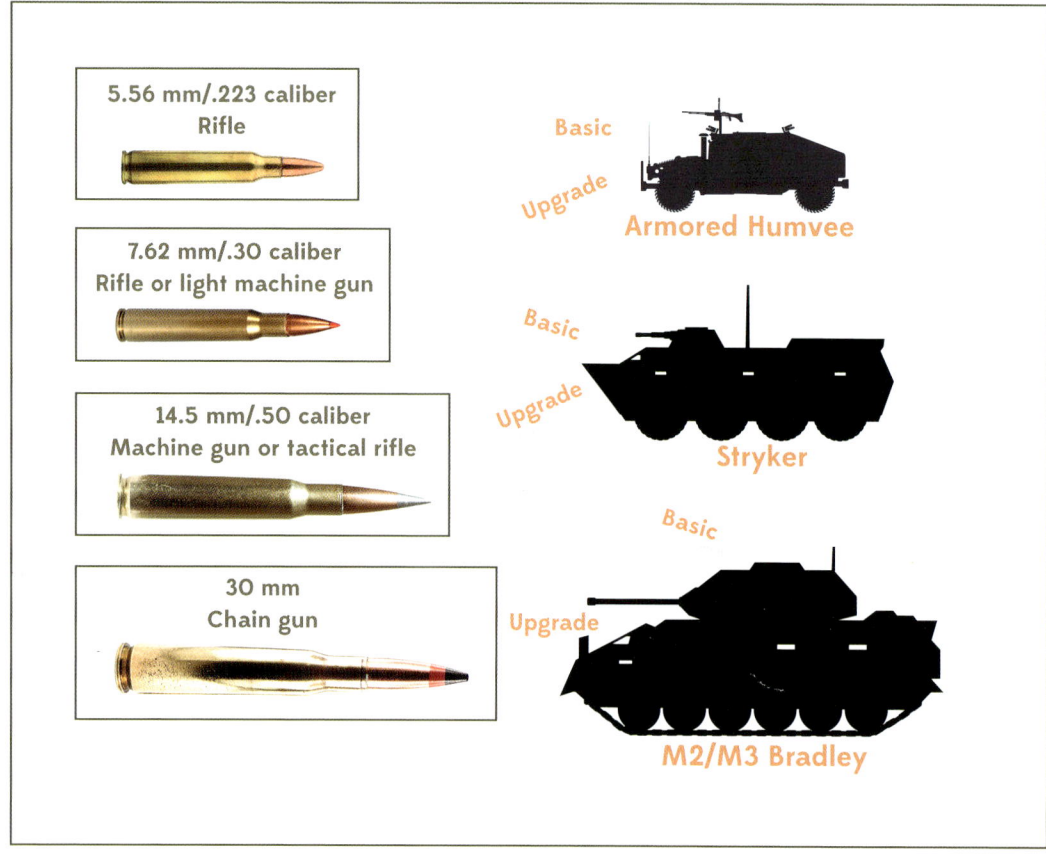

Providing Protection
The Humvee, the Stryker, and the Bradley offer different levels of protection against automatic weapons fire. This diagram shows the levels of firepower the basic and upgraded versions of each can withstand. How does this information compare with what you learned from the text? How is it similar? How is it different?

The US military uses many different types of vehicles to get the job done. Some have tracks, while others have wheels. Some are so large they can crush enemy defenses. Others are small enough to go through the thickest jungles. Yet all of the vehicles are designed to defeat the enemy while protecting the soldiers as much as possible. And as weapons and warfare continue to change, the vehicles will too.

FURTHER EVIDENCE

Chapter Four covers military vehicles with wheels, including the Humvee. What is the main point of this chapter? What key evidence supports this point? The article at the website below discusses a dangerous situation for soldiers in a Humvee. It also tells about an invention that helps them get to safety. Choose a quote from the article that relates to the chapter. Does the quote support the author's main point? Does it make a new point? Write a few sentences explaining your answer.

Making the Humvee Safer
www.mycorelibrary.com/vehicles

TOP MISSIONS

The Battle of 73 Easting

Some areas of Iraq are open desert. The military marked locations in these areas with lines on a coordinate grid. One of these lines was called 73 Easting. On February 26, 1991, Eagle Troop was advancing toward this line. This unit from the US Army's Second Armored Cavalry Regiment was part of a mission to take out divisions of the Iraqi Republican Guard.

Soldiers load into an M2 Bradley infantry fighting vehicle.

Eagle Troop's vehicles included nine M1A1 Abrams tanks and 13 M3A2 Bradley cavalry fighting vehicles. The troops moved on and passed over the 73 Easting line. When Eagle Troop crossed a ridge, they realized enemy tanks and armored vehicles were just ahead.

Commanding an M1A1 Abrams, Captain H. R. McMaster ordered his gunner to fire. In less than eight seconds, three enemy tanks were destroyed. But the Iraqis didn't fire back. McMaster realized they were facing the wrong way. The Iraqis weren't ready for combat.

McMaster made a quick decision. His troops were in the perfect position to attack. McMaster radioed the information, then gave the order. Two other units also attacked. In about an hour, Eagle Troop had destroyed more than 30 tanks and dozens of armored personnel carriers and trucks. On the American side, only one M3 Bradley was destroyed.

The Thunder Runs

Early in the second Iraq War (2003–2011) it became clear the United States would have to capture the capital city, Baghdad. Colonel David Perkins made a bold decision. On April 5, 2003, Perkins led the Third Mechanized Infantry Division in the First Thunder Run. Twenty-nine Abrams, 14 Bradleys, and various other vehicles swept into the city and out again, creating as much chaos as they could. As the American tanks rolled downtown, they hit the Iraqis hard and fast. Up to 3,000 enemy troops were killed.

Colonel David Perkins

Two days later, Colonel Perkins went back into Baghdad on the Second Thunder Run. With 70 Abrams and 60 Bradleys, the troops seized bridges and intersections. Just outside the city, they took control of the roads. The fight continued for four hours. To save fuel, Perkins had the men shut off the tank engines and operate them on battery power.

There were other problems too. The US control center was hit with a missile, and some of the soldiers were running out of ammunition. But the US troops held on. Supply trucks eventually made it through, and the area was secured.

STOP AND THINK

Say What?
Many military vehicles are referred to by their initials. Find five of these names. What do the initials stand for? Write the complete names and describe the vehicles.

Another View
This book has a lot of different examples of military vehicles. As you know, every source is different. Ask a librarian or another adult to help you find another source about military vehicles. Write a paragraph comparing and contrasting the two sources.

Why Do I Care?

You're not a soldier, and you're not fighting in a war. How does learning about military vehicles affect you? Does it change your view of soldiers and the military? If so, how?

Surprise Me

Chapters Three and Four identify different types of military vehicles used in the armed forces today. Which vehicles did you find the most surprising? Write a few sentences about each one and why you found it surprising.

GLOSSARY

armor
protective covering used to prevent damage to a vehicle

artillery fragments
pieces of a bursting artillery shell

bunker
a military fortification usually belowground

convoy
a group of vehicles traveling together for protection

deployed
put to use

embankment
a raised bank or wall

hull
the frame or body of a vehicle, ship, or aircraft

kill zone
an area in a battle where many soldiers are killed

maneuver
to move smoothly and skillfully

reconnaissance
to go into enemy territory to gain information

small arms fire
bullets from a gun that can be carried in one hand

winch
a machine that winds a rope, cable, or chain on a roller to lift or pull heavy objects

LEARN MORE

Books

Adams, Simon. *Soldier*. New York: DK Children, 2009.

Hamilton, John. *Abrams Tanks*. Minneapolis, MN: Abdo Publishing, 2011.

Perritano, John, and James Spears. *National Geographic Kids: Everything Battles*. Washington, DC: National Geographic Children's Books, 2013.

Websites

To learn more about the US military and its resources, visit **booklinks.abdopublishing.com**. These links are routinely monitored and updated to provide the most current information available.

Visit **www.mycorelibrary.com** for free additional tools for teachers and students.

INDEX

Abrams Main Battle Tanks, 22–25, 27, 28, 29
Afghanistan, 25
Amphibious Assault Vehicles, 5

Baghdad, Iraq, 5, 10
Benz, Karl, 14
Bradley Infantry Fighting Vehicles, 25–28, 40
Bradley, Omar, 27

Chontosh, Brian, 6–11

Desert Patrol Vehicles, 38

FANG Challenge, 36
Ford, Henry, 14
Ford Model T, 14
Franklin, Thomas, 6, 8, 11

Gulf War, 5–11, 22, 25, 31

half-track vehicles, 17
HERCULES, 28–31
Humvees, 5–11, 33–34, 38, 40, 41

Iraq, 5–10, 25, 31

jeeps, 13, 16, 18, 19, 34

Kerman, Robert, 6, 8
Korte, Ken, 6, 8

M35 cargo truck, 18–19
McCormick, Armand, 6, 8–9, 11
Mechanical Mule, 17–18
Mighty Mite, 18
MRAPs, 37–39

Nash Quad, 14–15

Stryker Infantry Carrier Vehicles, 35–36, 40

Vietnam War, 17, 18

World War I, 14–15, 16
World War II, 15–19, 27

ABOUT THE AUTHOR

Samantha Bell lives in the upstate of South Carolina with her family and lots of animals. She is the author and/or illustrator of more than 20 books for children. She is thankful for those who have served and are currently serving in the US military.